D0520662

J6

FAST FREDDIE FROG

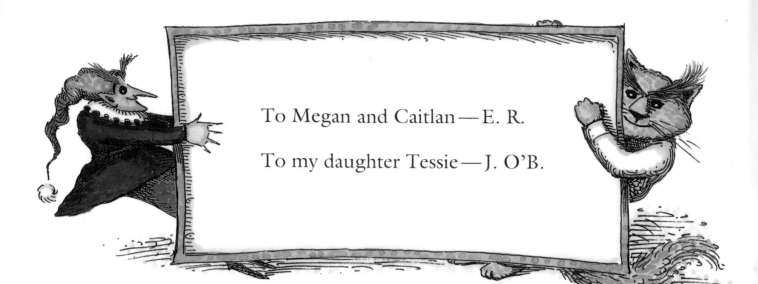

To Megan and Caitlan—E. R.

To my daughter Tessie—J. O'B.

*Author's Note: I have made most of the rhymes in this book
from prose originals in our folklore.*

Published by Caroline House
Boyds Mills Press, Inc.
A Highlights Company
910 Church Street
Honesdale, Pennsylvania 18431

Publisher Cataloging-in-Publication Data
Rees, Ennis.
Fast Freddie Frog and other tongue-twister rhymes / by Ennis Rees;
illustrated by John O'Brien.—1st ed.
[32] p. : col. ill. ; cm.
Summary: A collection of hard-to-say humorous rhymes, accompanied by
cartoon-style illustrations.
ISBN 1-56397-038-4
1. Tongue twisters—Juvenile literature. 2. Humorous poetry —Juvenile literature.
[1. Tongue twisters. 2. Humorous poetry.] I. O'Brien, John, ill. II. Title.
818.54—dc20   1993
Library of Congress Catalog Card Number: 92-81077

First edition, 1993
Book designed by Katy Riegel
The text of this book is set in 18-point Galliard.
The illustrations are done in pen and ink, dyes, and watercolors.
Distributed by St. Martin's Press
Printed in the United States of America

1   3   5   7   9   10   8   6   4   2

FAST FREDDIE FROG

and other Tongue-Twister Rhymes

BY **ENNIS REES**

ILLUSTRATED BY **JOHN O'BRIEN**

When will the seething sea
Cease seething ceaselessly?

CAROLINE HOUSE

BOYDS MILLS PRESS

He ran on Sundays.
He ran on Mondays.
He ran from the Indies to the Andes
In his undies.

Frivolous Fanny
 Fried fresh fish
For four famished Frenchmen
 Acting child-ish.

If a beagle baked cakes and bagels
Out by the loony lake,
How many cakes and bagels
Could the baking beagle bake?

Elfish Sue,
Unselfish Sue,
Loves to dine
On selfish shellfish.

"This is my sister's zither, mister,"
Said Thomas to Dr. Fell,
But it was Thomas's *twin* sisters' zither,
And both of them played it well.

The sailor's tailor,
Merrily,
Failed furling and failed
Thoroughly.

Pop dropped the slop mop
By the puddle of glop
When the cop stopped to hop.

Wood said he would carry the wood
 As far as he could through the wood,
And if Wood said he would carry the wood,
 Wood would.

Nick the knocker
Nightly knocks knickknacks.
No knickknack knocker
Knocks knickknacks like Nick
The nightly knickknack knocker.

Sheep shouldn't
Sleep in a sack.

Sheep shouldn't
Sleep in a bed.

Sheep shouldn't
Sleep in a shack.

Sheep should
Sleep in a shed.

Mack Yak
    Never lacks.
Mack Yak
    Packs sacks.

Fast Freddie Frog,
    He flips 'em in a dish.
Fast Freddie Frog
    Fries flat flying fish.

Lucky Louie Lion,
    He skips and then he hops.
Then Lucky Louie Lion licks
    His lemon lollipops.

Like a greedy feaster
   Shaking on his legs,
Eddie every Easter
   Eats eighty Easter eggs.

Bobo shook
   His brown head sadly
When Barbara burned
   The black bread badly.

Which witch wished
The wicked wish?
Which witch mixed
The magical dish?

Hairy Harry Hartley
Hurried on to Rome.
Then Hairy Harry Hartley
Hurried home.

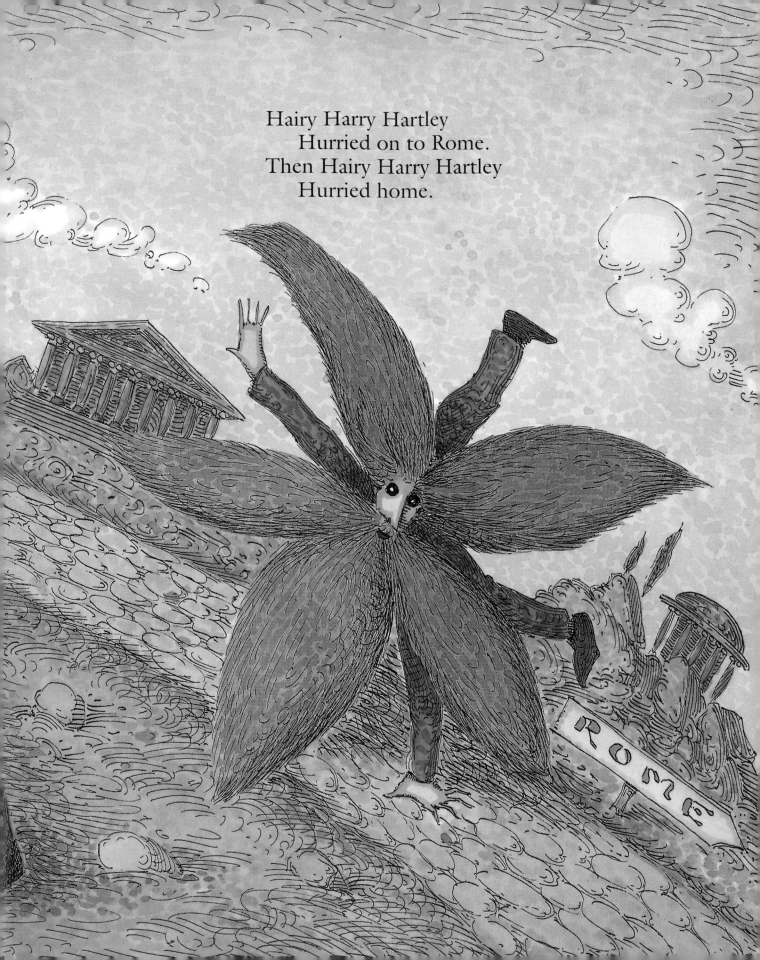

Prissy Peacock, pink and proud,
Prissy Peacock fumes.
Then Prissy Peacock pompously
Preens her pretty plumes.

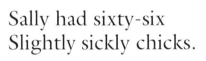

Sally had sixty-six
Slightly sickly chicks.

Joe jumps in January,
    So cold it makes him cry.
But Joe jumps joyfully
    In June and July.

Ten tomcats tottering
    In the tops of three tall trees
Are ten truly terrified tomcats
    Tumbling around in the breeze.

Round and round the ragged rocks
　　Now runs the rugged man,
Where round and round the rugged rocks
　　The ragged rascal ran.

My wooden whistle wouldn't whistle,
So I bought a shiny steel whistle.
But my steel whistle steel wouldn't whistle,
So I bought a tiny tin whistle,
And now I tin whistle.

Happy Henry Hippo hops—
    "Look out!" we scream. "He's coming!"
And Happy Henry Hippo hops
    Over a high hill humming.

Some shun sunshine,
    Without any doubt,
But though some do shun sunshine,
    Others seek it out.

Whenever you come
   To a bit of trouble,
Remember that Double Bubble gum
   Bubbles double.

If you go to France
Maybe you'll see
Five French friars fanning
A fainted flea.

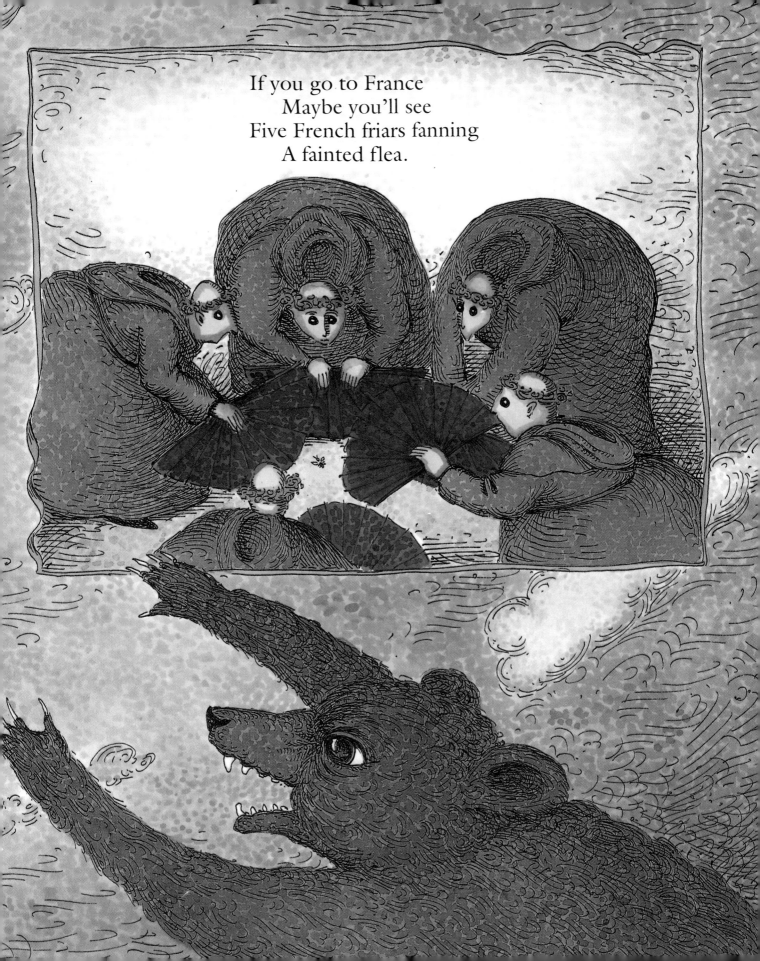

The four fat fellows,
Precociously,
Went at their fiddling
Ferociously.

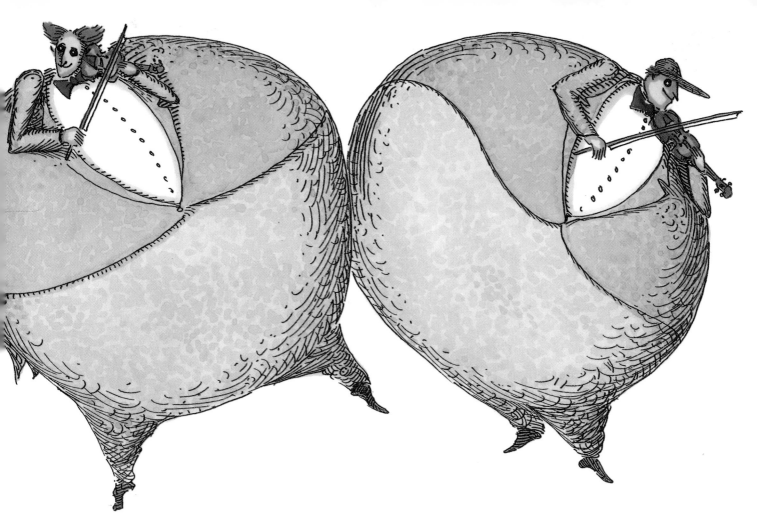

Sue says she sews shirts seriously,
She says she sews shirts sadly,
But she must sew shirts deliriously
To twist our tongues so badly.

The storm is over,
  We're still breathing,
And the seething sea
  Ceaseth seething.